Other books about
Stinkbomb & Ketchup-Face:

These books are almost as magical as me!

Stinkbomb & Ketchup-Face and the Badness of Badgers

Stinkbomb & Ketchup-Face and the Quest for the Magic Porcupine

Stinkbomb & Ketchup-Face and the Evilness of Pizza

Stinkbomb & Ketchup-Face and the Bees of Stupidity

Stinkbomb & Ketchup-Face and the Great Big Story Nickers

John Dougherty

Stinkbomb & Ketchup-Face

and the Great Kerfuffle Christmas Kidnap

Illustrated by
David Tazzyman
(Illustrator of
Mr Gum)

OXFORD
UNIVERSITY PRESS

OXFORD
UNIVERSITY PRESS

Great Clarendon Street, Oxford OX2 6DP
Oxford University Press is a department of the University of Oxford.
It furthers the University's objective of excellence in research, scholarship,
and education by publishing worldwide. Oxford is a registered
trade mark of Oxford University Press in the UK and in certain other countries

Text © John Dougherty 2016
Inside illustrations © David Tazzyman 2016
The moral rights of the author and illustrator have been asserted
Ketchup splat image by Pjorg/Shutterstock.com
Illustrative font on page 171 © Sudtipos

Database right Oxford University Press (maker)

First published 2016

British Library Cataloguing in Publication Data

Data available

ISBN: 978-0-19-274778-5

1 3 5 7 9 10 8 6 4 2

Printed in Great Britain
Paper used in the production of this book is a natural,
recyclable product made from wood grown in sustainable forests
The manufacturing process conforms to the environmental
regulations of the country of origin

As always and ever, for Noah and Cara,
with love and mince pies 'cos it's Christmas.

And Merry Christmas, everybody! J.D.

For Millie and Izzy. D.T.

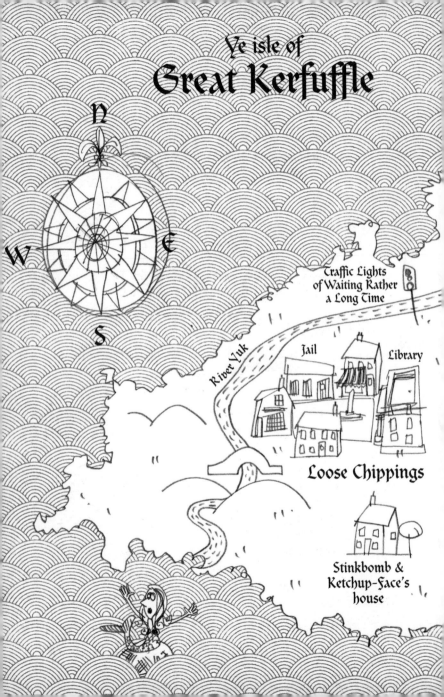

Enchanted
Wood

Stupidity

Volcano
of Death

Mountains
of Doom

Swamp
of Misery

Stream

Valley of Despair

Asillyname

REPORT ON THE CITIZENS OF GREAT KERFUFFLE, BY JINGLE, HELPFUL WORKSHOP ELF NO. 37:

STINKBOMB

- **DESCRIPTION:**
  Boy. Sort of boy-sized.

- **WHAT HE'D LIKE FOR CHRISTMAS:**
  Useful things to keep in his pockets.

- **RECOMMENDATION:**
  One of those penknives with 47 different attachments.

- **WHICH LIST:**
  The Nice List. Definitely.

KETCHUP-FACE

- **DESCRIPTION:**
  Girl. Smaller than Stinkbomb.

- **WHAT SHE'D LIKE FOR CHRISTMAS:**
  A beautiful horsey.

- **RECOMMENDATION:**
  Something she can pretend is a beautiful horsey.

- **WHICH LIST:**
  Without a doubt, the Nice List.

KING TOOTHBRUSH WEASEL

- **DESCRIPTION:**
  King. Though somehow less kingly
  than the average king.

- **WHAT HE'D LIKE FOR CHRISTMAS:**
  Fresh tinsel to make his throne look
  a bit more throney.

- **RECOMMENDATION:**
  A big book with lots of correctly-labelled pictures of animals.

- **WHICH LIST:**
  Do we have a Stupid List?
  If not, the Nice List.

MALCOLM THE CAT

- **DESCRIPTION:**
  Cat. Small, grey, and wearing a red
  soldier's jacket because he is the army.

- **WHAT HE'D LIKE FOR CHRISTMAS:**
  Anything tormentable.

- **RECOMMENDATION:**
  A big tin of cat food. And a tin opener, if he's been good.

- **WHICH LIST:**
  The Nice List.
        Or perhaps the Naughty List.

                Though maybe the Nice List would be better.

                        But then again . . .

MISS BUTTERWORTH

- **DESCRIPTION:**
  Ninja Librarian.

- **WHAT SHE'D LIKE FOR CHRISTMAS:**
  World peace, universal harmony,
  and an end to overdue library books.

- **RECOMMENDATION:**
  A sword cosy to keep her big sword warm in the winter.

- **WHICH LIST:**
  The Wise List, if we've got one.
  If not, the Nice List.

THE LITTLE SHOPPING TROLLEY

- **DESCRIPTION:**
  Shopping trolley. Little.

- **WHAT IT WOULD LIKE FOR CHRISTMAS:**
  The day off.

- **RECOMMENDATION:**
  A nice tin of wheel polish.

- **WHICH LIST:**
  The Nice List.

THE BADGERS

- **DESCRIPTION:**
  Badgers. You know: black and grey and white,
  a bit stripey, that sort of thing.

- **WHAT THEY'D LIKE FOR CHRISTMAS:**
  Anything to help them do evil and wicked doings.

- **RECOMMENDATION:**
  DO NOT GIVE THEM ANYTHING TO HELP THEM DO
  EVIL AND WICKED DOINGS.

- **WHICH LIST:**
  The evil and wicked list.

Chapter 1

In which the badgers hatch an evil and wicked plan

'Twas the night before Christmas
And all through the prison
Not a creature was stirring
Except for the badgers . . .

It was Christmas Eve on the little island of Great
Kerfuffle. The stars shone pin-bright, each one
a miniature jewel on the deep blue velvet cloth of
the night sky. A crisp new coat of frost glistened on
the ground. Flakes of snow were beginning to fall

through the wintry air, glittering in the moonlight like the dandruff of angels.

And in the jail in the tiny village of Loose Chippings, the badgers were complaining.

'Bother,' said Rolf the Badger, a big badger with a big badge that said (Big Badger). 'It looks like we're going to be spending Christmas in prison. I don't want to spend Christmas in prison.'

'Yeah,' agreed Harry the Badger, taking a sip of tea from a mug marked (World's Best Badger). 'How are we going to have an **evil** and **wicked** Christmas if we're in prison?'

'At least Father Christmas will know where to find us,' said Stewart the Badger, the smallest of the badgers, hanging up a stocking next to the fireplace. 'I wonder what he'll bring? I hope I get something nice for Christmas!'

'I know what I want for Christmas,'

said Harry the Badger, stroking his badgery chin in what he hoped was an **evil** and **wicked** yet stylish manner. 'I want to escape from prison. Has anyone got any ideas how?'

'We could ask Father Christmas to bring us a digger,' suggested Stewart the Badger. 'And then we could drive it too fast and dig our way out of prison!'

Harry the Badger rolled his eyes scornfully. 'And how would Father Christmas get a digger into the prison?'

'Down the chimney!' said Stewart the Badger cheerfully.

Rolf the Badger went to the fireplace and stuck his head **up** the chimney. 'Nope,' he said. 'You'd never get a digger **down** the chimney. It's not even big enough for a badger.'

'Well,' said Stewart the Badger, 'Father Christmas comes down the chimney. And he's **bigger** than a badger. And he brings a **big** bag of **presents** with him. And *that's* **bigger** than a badger. So I think he *could* bring a digger.'

Rolf the Badger scratched his head. 'How does he do that, then? I mean, he's not exactly thin.'

'No,' said Stewart the Badger in an explaining sort of voice, 'but he's magic.'

'Hang on a minute,' said Harry the Badger in a having-an-idea sort of voice. 'Yeah. He's magic. He must be. He must have some kind of magic that can get him and the **presents** **up** and **down** chimneys . . . '

'Maybe he is,' said Rolf the Badger, in a not-quite-getting-it-yet sort of voice, 'but how does that help us escape?'

❅   ❅   ❅

The snow was falling faster now. It fell in moonlit flurries that **danced** around the chimney-pots and **whirled** between the rooftops. And in the distance, through the darkness and the **spiralling** snow, something moved across the sky. Something **big**, and fast, and magical. Silent hooves **beat** against the air; gentle bells **jingled** on soft leather harnesses. Somebody **laughed**: a deep, joyful, heartwarming sound. A **clatter** of reindeer on the roof; the **swish** of the sleigh's runners. Boots **crunched** through the snow towards the prison chimney, and someone much too large to fit slipped inside it with supernatural ease.

Moments later, inside the prison, a puff of soot blew out onto the hearth and Father Christmas stood there, large as life and twice as jolly. 'Now then,' he muttered.

'What did I bring for those badgers ... ?'

And then he stopped, and scratched his head in puzzlement; for the jail was empty of badgers. There was nothing there except a large number of badly-wrapped **Christmas presents**.

'Well, bless my soul!' said Father Christmas. 'What are all these **presents** doing here already? If they *are* **presents**, that is . . . '

'Oh,' said one of the **presents**, 'we're **presents**, all right. That's why we're all wrapped up in Christmas wrapping paper like this.'

'You're not very *well* wrapped,' said Father Christmas suspiciously. 'Are you *sure* you're **presents?**'

'Oh, yes,' said the **present** earnestly. 'We're definitely **presents**. We're very **presenty** indeed. Isn't that right, Rolf the Present?'

'That's right,' agreed Rolf the Present, a **big present** with a big badge that said $\begin{pmatrix} Big \\ Present \end{pmatrix}$. 'We're **presents** all right. Aren't we, Harry the Present?'

'Yes,' agreed Harry the Present, taking a sip of

tea from a mug marked, [World's Best Present]. 'We're extremely **presenty**. Aren't we, Stewart the Present?'

Just as Stewart the Present was opening his mouth to answer, Harry the Present passed him a note that said:

Pretend we're presents.

Stewart the Present read it slowly three times and then said, 'Er, we're **presents**.' He turned the note over. On the other side it said:

Don't let them know we're badgers.

'Er, we're not badgers,' he added.

'Oh,' said Father Christmas uncertainly. 'Um . . . All right, then. So what are you doing here already? *I* didn't bring you.'

'Yes, you did!' said Harry the Present quickly. 'You brought us . . . um . . . last year. Isn't that right, **presents?**'

'Oh, yes,' said all the other **presents**, nodding.

'Only . . . only the badgers had already been let out of prison for being good,' Harry the Present went on. 'So they never got to open us. But,' he went on persuasively, 'if you take us in your sleigh, then you can give us to the badgers when you find them.'

'Oh,' said Father Christmas again. 'Well . . . this is most unusual. I don't think I've ever taken **presents** back **up** the chimney before. But then, I've never got anybody's address wrong, either. I really don't know how this has happened. All right, in you hop.'

He opened his sack, and all the **presents** hopped inside, stifling **evil** and **wicked** laughs as they did so.

chapter 2

In which Stinkbomb and Ketchup-Face wake up
and discover that all is not as it should be

The snow had stopped falling now, and lay thick and white upon the ground. The little island of Great Kerfuffle slept beneath the bright moon.

And in a tall tree in the garden of a lovely house high on a hillside above the tiny village of Loose Chippings, a blackbird wasn't singing. Nor was it playing a trumpet or **banging** an enormous drum.

It was sleeping on a branch, dressed in an owl costume.

Inside the lovely house, in a beautiful pink bedroom, a little girl called Ketchup-Face woke suddenly from her dreams. Leaping from her bed, she ran to the window, flung open the shutters, and yelled,

'Oi! Blackbird!!!!
Shut your...'

She stopped. There was no **singing**, or **trumpeting**, or **banging**, though she had dreamed that there was. There was only the silence of the snow-covered night, and the brightness of the stars, and the suspiciously blackbirdy snoring of the owl in the nearby tree.

Ketchup-Face rubbed her eyes, and blinked. But there was no doubt: she was awake, in the middle of the night, and there wasn't even a black-bird she could be cross with,

and . . . and . . .

and . . .

It was

CHRIST

15

Her head suddenly full of Christmas cheer and goodwill, she scooped a load of snow off her window sill, raced with it across the landing to her brother's room, and dumped it down his neck.

'Wake up, Stinkbomb!'

she shouted.

'IT'S CHRI

Stinkbomb had already woken up. The moment the snow had been dumped down his neck, he had gone from very asleep to very awake without passing through any of the usual stages in between.

'Yeep!' he said, shaking himself and doing a funny little **hoppity** dance all round the room. 'Wh-wh-wh-what did you do that for?'

'BECAUSE IT'S CHRISTMAS!!!!!!!'

Ketchup-Face explained, doing her own little **hoppity** dance because she was so excited. 'And the story's started! And it's all very mysterious. There wasn't a blackbird, and it's the middle of the night, and . . . Stinkbomb! It's been snowing!!!

AND IT'S CHRISTMAS!!!!'

They stared at one another for a moment, eyes wide.

'Christmas!' breathed Stinkbomb, and looked at the clock. 'It's . . . **Chapter Two**.' He paused, and scratched his head. 'I wonder if Father Christmas has been yet? Hang on.'

He picked up his shorts from where they had been carelessly dropped on the floor, and fumbled around in the pocket, producing after a moment or two a clock shaped like a Christmas tree. It was showing a time somewhere between 'Father Christmas comes' and 'Wake your parents ridiculously early'.

'He's been!!!' exclaimed Stinkbomb. Ketchup-Face took up the cry, and shouting, 'He's been! He's been! He's been!' the pair of them hurried down the stairs and into the living-room, where, under the Christmas tree, they found a great **big** pile of . . .

. . . nothing.

Nothing at all.

And their stockings, which they had left hanging on the mantelpiece, were limp and empty.

Chapter 3

In which it becomes clear that something is very wrong with Christmas

Stinkbomb checked the Christmas clock again.

'He should definitely have been by now,' he said worriedly.

Ketchup-Face's lip began to tremble. 'What if something's happened to him?' she asked. 'Maybe he's had an accident.'

'I don't think he *has* accidents,' said Stinkbomb.

'Well, *something's* happened,' said Ketch-up-Face. 'He can't just have missed us! We've been really good this year!'

'Really really good,' agreed Stinkbomb. 'I mean—all else aside, just think how many times we've thwarted the badgers!'

'Yes,' said Ketchup-Face. 'Something *must* have happened to him.'

Stinkbomb scratched his head. 'I know! Let's look at the Santa-Tracker website!'

They went to the computer, looked up the Santa-Tracker website, and pressed the 'track Santa' button. Instead of the map they were expecting, two faces—a man and a woman—appeared on the screen. They looked like very serious newsreaders.

'Well,' said the man, 'this is most troubling, isn't it, Connie?'

'It certainly is, Jim,' said the woman. 'Santa Claus—also known as Father Christmas—hasn't been seen for over an hour. Our satellites have completely lost track of him.'

'Remind us, Connie,' said Jim, 'where Santa was last seen.'

'Well, Jim, he was last seen entering the airspace of a little island known as Great Kerfuffle.'

'But, Connie—isn't Great Kerfuffle a fictional island?'

'It certainly is, Jim. Which means that Santa Claus is currently missing inside a story.'

Jim looked worried. 'Then it's up to the heroes of that story—whoever they are—to rescue Santa Claus . . . '

'That's right, Jim. But whether they call him Santa Claus, or Father Christmas—if they don't rescue him very soon, then Christmas is in serious danger!'

The video faded to black, with some artful snowflakes over the top.

Stinkbomb looked at his sister. Her jaw was set in a determined manner.

'Stinkbomb,' she said, 'something has happened to Father Christmas. And it's up to us to rescue him. Connie and Jim said so.'

'Well,' said Stinkbomb. 'In that case, it must be true! Let's go!'

And they went.

After getting dressed, of course.

Chapter 4

In which Stinkbomb and Ketchup-Face
have trouble with snow

'**Wheeeeee!**' Ketchup-Face
yelled, dashing out into the wintry night.

'**Glumph!!!!!**'

she added, disappearing into the deep snowdrift
outside the front door and getting snow up her nose.

'What does "glumph" mean?' Stinkbomb
asked.

'**Glumph!!!!!**'

25

he went on, as he emerged from the house and disappeared into the snowdrift next to his sister. 'Oooof!' he continued, clambering out again.

'Oooof!' Ketchup-Face agreed. 'Why is there so much snow?'

'There is a lot, isn't there,' Stinkbomb said. 'I expect it's because this is a Christmas story. There's always lots of snow in a Christmas story.'

'I do like snow,' said Ketchup-Face, standing up. 'Glumph!!!!!' she added, disappearing into the snowdrift again.

'Hang on,' Stinkbomb told her, fishing around in his pocket. 'I think I might have some snow-shoes somewhere. Yes, here they are!' he said, pulling out four tennis racquets. 'Oh. Those aren't snowshoes...' He fumbled about some more, and produced four tennis racquets with straps on.

'Is that what snowshoes are?' Ketchup-Face asked curiously, popping **up** out of the snowdrift once more.

'I think so,' Stinkbomb said. 'Oh, look. There's a note on one of them.'

There was. It said:

Dear Stinkbomb & Ketchup-Face

I'm afraid I've never actually seen a pair of snowshoes, let alone worn them; but I've seen lots of cartoons and comic strips set in the snow, and snowshoes always look like tennis racquets in those, so I hope this is right.

Lots of love
The writer

Tennis racquet

straps to tie to shoes

'Oh,' said Stinkbomb. 'Well . . . I suppose we ought to try them.'

'I expect they'll work,' Ketchup-Face said. 'If the writer's put them in the story, they ought to.'

'Not necessarily,' said Stinkbomb. 'Writers put things in a story for all kinds of reasons. Maybe they'll help us solve a problem later on. Maybe they'll even cause a problem!'

'Do you think so?' Ketchup-Face asked, eyeing the snowshoes nervously. 'What sort of problem? Do you think they might eat us?'

'I doubt it,' Stinkbomb said wisely. 'I don't think the writer would let us get eaten by snow-shoes. Unless it was *really* funny. Oh, look—there's another note!'

And there was, stuck to another of the snow-shoes. Stinkbomb peeled it off and read it. It said:

PS. Please stop talking about snowshoes and get on with the story.

'Oh,' said Stinkbomb. 'OK.'
And they did.

chapter 5

In which Stinkbomb and Ketchup-Face get on with the story

It took them several attempts to get the snowshoes on. This was partly because it wasn't easy to see how the straps did up; and partly because Ketch-up-Face kept using them to hit snowballs over the washing line. But eventually they put them on, and were on their way.

There was something magical about being outside in the moonlit darkness, in the snow, on the night of Christmas Eve. The midnight earth seemed enchanted; and as Ketchup-Face glanced upwards, she gasped. 'Stinkbomb!' she said, her voice filled with awe. 'The stars are so **big!** See how they're **twinkling** and **blinking**! And . . . and they're all the colours of the rainbow!'

'Er . . . no,' said Stinkbomb. 'Those aren't the stars. You put **fairy lights** round your hat to make it more Christmassy. Remember?'

'Oh,' said Ketchup-Face, taking off her hat and looking at it. 'Yeah. I forgot.'

On they walked, their snowshoes **crunching** on the deep snow, marvelling at how all of nature seemed to be celebrating the season of goodwill. The frosted trees **glistened** and **glittered**; icicles hung from their boughs like candy canes, and stars rested in their upper branches. Frozen berries **glinted** like glass baubles on the bushes. In a scene that could have come straight from a Christmas card, a robin perched gracefully on a snow-covered log beneath the words *Seasons Greetings*. They saw a fox in a novelty Santa hat, and a majestic stag wearing comedy Christmas antlers on top of its antlers. A magnificent snowy owl swooped low, resplendent in its **tinsel** scarf and cheerful Christmas onesie; a turkey waddled past, carrying a nut roast home from the shops.

The calm was broken by a strange, unearthly sound. It came from above them; but they could not tell exactly where, for it seemed to be moving at great speed.

And then, suddenly, something huge and dark loomed out of the sky. At enormous speed the creature, whatever it was, swooped at them, making a horrible noise that sounded like:

'AAAAAAAAAAAAARGH!'

'DUCK!'

yelled Stinkbomb, throwing himself on top of his sister just in time. 'Glumph!!!!!' he added, getting a faceful of snow as he hit the ground.

'Glumph!!!!!' Ketchup-Face agreed. She looked up at where the thing was disappearing into the night, and wiped her mouth. 'That wasn't a duck! Ducks are smaller. And they go **Quack**, not AAAAAAAAAAAARGH!!!!!!!!!!!'

'No,' explained Stinkbomb, as they got to their feet. 'When I said *duck*, I meant: *get your head as low as you can, as quickly as possible, out of the way of danger, in much the same way that a duck lowers its head in a fast dipping motion when it's searching for food under water.*'

'Oh,' said Ketchup-Face. 'Why didn't you say so?'

'Because it's a bit long,' Stinkbomb said. 'By the time I'd finished, that thing would have bopped us on the heads, or carried us away to its lair, or something. It's much quicker just to say *DUCK!*'

'Yes, I suppose it is,' agreed Ketchup-Face.

'NO!'

said Stinkbomb urgently,

'I MEAN ACTUALLY

DUCK!!!!'
oooo

And he threw himself on top of his sister again,
causing them both to go 'Glumph!!!!!' just
as the mysterious thing, with its unearthly cry of

'AAAAAAAAAAARGH!!!!!!!!!'
oooooooo

swooped out of the sky once more and almost bopped them on the heads or carried them off to its lair or something.

They raised their heads and looked, as the mysterious creature shot back into the air at incredible speed. They could see it only in silhouette against the light of the moon, but even so they could tell it was like nothing they had ever seen before. It had a large, long body, and several bizarrely-shaped heads. Strangest of all was its tail, which looked like nothing so much as a badger clinging on with one front paw while the other front paw firmly clutched a mug of tea. Oddly, the

'AAAAAAAAAAAAARGH

noise appeared to be coming from the tail, while the heads were making another, fainter noise: a noise that sounded like sleigh bells **jingling** in the way you might expect them to **jingle** if they were attached to the harnesses of a lot of magical reindeer which were a bit frightened but mostly rather cross.

❄   ❄   ❄

'What was it?' Ketchup-Face asked, staring after the thing.

Stinkbomb scratched his head. 'If I didn't know better, I'd say it looked like a magic sleigh pulled by flying reindeer with a badger hanging off the back.'

Ketchup-Face looked at him, and then back at the sky, where the mysterious thing was climbing **higher** and **higher**, faster and faster. 'Don't be silly,' she said. 'How likely is *that*?'

They watched as, far above them, the thing looped the loop—conveniently, just in front of the moon where they could see it really clearly. It shot across the sky once more; and as it passed high above their heads, it drew its badger-shaped tail in, and something fell from it.

Down it fell,

down, down,

down . . .

'Um . . . Do you think we should get out of the way?' asked Ketchup-Face.

'Good idea,' said Stinkbomb; and they both stepped to one side as the falling object plummeted into the thick snow just next to them.

chapter 6

'Did the flying thing lay an egg?' Ketchup-Face asked.

'I don't think it's an egg,' Stinkbomb answered, looking curiously at the new arrival, which was half-buried in the snow. It was roundish in shape and brown in colour, apart from the two shiny black bits at the top. If you hadn't known better, you might have said it looked like a big sack with a pair of boots sticking out.

'What *is* it, then?' said Ketchup-Face curiously, laying a gentle hand on it.

The object groaned, and **wriggled**.

'Stinkbomb!' Ketchup-Face said. 'It's alive! It's some kind of animal!'

The object **wriggled** again, and made a noise that sounded like, `Hmmmp! Hmmmp!'

'Isn't she lovely!' said Ketchup-Face. 'I'm going to keep her as a pet. I shall call her . . . Sacky!'

'Should we turn it the right way up, do you think?' Stinkbomb asked.

'She *is* the right way up,' said Ketchup-Face. 'Her ears are sticking out the top.'

'Um . . . I think those are its feet,' said Stink-bomb.

'Oh,' said Ketchup-Face. '*I* think they're her ears.'

'They look like feet to me,' said Stinkbomb.

They paused for a moment, and regarded the creature.

'Well,' said Ketchup-Face, 'let's ask her. Excuse me, Sacky, but are you the right way up?'

Sacky **wriggled**, and made a noise that sounded like, 'Nmmmm.'

'Are you the *wrong way* up?' asked Stinkbomb.

'Ymmmmm! Ymmmm!'

the creature said.

'That doesn't help,' said Ketchup-Face. 'I know! I'll sing a Christmas song in her ears, and if they're really her feet they'll start dancing.' And she cleared her throat and began to sing:

'Jingle bells
   Jingle bells
  Jingle jingle bells!

  Jingle jingle jingle jingle

   Jingle jingle bells

OH!

Jingle bells
   Jingle bells
  Jingle jingle bells
 Jingle jingle jingle jingle jingle jingle bells!!!!'

As she sang, the black bootish-looking bits sticking out of the top began to jiggle and kick furiously— so much so that by the time she had stopped and added, 'That's a song about **jingle bells!** Stinkbomb, with a good solid push, had turned Sacky the other way up. It struggled to what now appeared to be its feet, and sank bottom-deep in the snow.

'Ah,' said Stinkbomb. 'I think, um, Sacky needs some snowshoes.' He fumbled around in his pocket and after some moments produced a tennis racquet and a couple of bits of string. 'I don't think I've got any snowshoes left,' he said. 'This will have to do.' And pulling Sacky's feet out of the snowdrift, he tied the tennis racquet to them.

It took Stinkbomb and Ketchup-Face several goes to get Sacky upright again—it really was quite heavy—but eventually the creature was standing precariously on its racquet-clad feet.

'Hmmmm,' said Ketchup-Face. 'I wonder where she came from?'

And as if in answer to that question, the story decided to go back and see what had happened to the badgers between their escape from prison in **Chapter One**, and the events of **Chapter Two**. .

In which we find out what happened
between chapter one and chapter two

'My goodness!' said Father Christmas, clamber-ing out of the prison chimney-stack. 'These **presents** are heavy.'

The presents stifled **evil** and **wicked** laughs as Father Christmas unloaded them from his sack.

'You know,' he said, 'you really are the most badly-wrapped **presents** I've ever come across. Are you *sure* I delivered you last year?'

'Oh, yes,' said all the **presents**, nodding earnestly.

'Well,' said Father Christmas, 'I think we ought to unwrap you and start again. We can't give you to the badgers looking like this.' And he unwrapped all the **presents**. 'Wait a minute!' he said.

'You are the badgers! Mmmmmph!!!!!ooooo'

he added, as the badgers shoved all the discarded wrapping paper in his mouth and popped the sack over his head. 'Hmmmmmp! Hmmmmmmmmmp!!!!' he continued, as they tied the neck of the sack tightly around his ankles and threw him in the back of the sleigh.

'What do we do now?' asked Rolf the Badger.

'What do you *think* we do now?!?' said Harry the Badger, leaping into the sleigh and grabbing

46

hold of the reins. 'I've always wanted to drive a magic sleigh too fast!'

'Yay!!!' said the other badgers, and they all crammed into the sleigh as Harry the Badger flicked the reins and said, 'Giddy-up!'

Nothing happened.

'Giddy-up!' Harry the Badger said again.

Still, nothing happened.

'Giddy-up, you stupid reindeer!' Harry the Badger snarled. 'Why aren't you giddying up?'

'Did you remember to take the handbrake off?' Rolf the Badger asked.

'Don't be stupid, Rolf the Badger!' Harry the Badger said. 'Magic sleighs don't have handbrakes!'

'Oh,' said Rolf the Badger.

'What does this lever do?' asked Stewart the Badger, pulling a lever.

'Whoooooooooooaaaaaaaaaaaaaaahhhhhhhhhhhhh!!!!!!!!!!!!!!!!!'

went all the badgers as, with a sudden **stamping** of reindeer hooves, the sleigh left the rooftop and shot into the sky. 'Wheeeeeeeeeee!' the badgers continued, as they realized it was actually rather fun.

'Har har har,' added Harry the Badger.

'Why are you laughing an **evil** and **wicked** laugh?' Stewart the Badger asked.

'Because, Stewart the Badger,' said Harry the Badger, 'this is probably the most **evil** and **wicked** thing we've ever done!'

'Oh, OK,' said Stewart the Badger. 'Er . . . what *have* we done, exactly?'

Harry the Badger rolled his eyes. 'What we've done, Stewart the Badger, is: we've kidnapped Father Christmas and stolen his sleigh! You don't get much **eviller** and **wickeder** than that!'

'Hur hur hur,' laughed Rolf the Badger **evilly** and **wickedly**. '*And* we're driving his sleigh too fast!'

'Yeah,' agreed Harry the Badger. 'If only there was a chicken we could frighten, as well.'

'We could frighten the reindeer,' Stewart the Badger suggested.

'Good idea, Stewart the Badger!' said Harry the Badger.

And they frightened the reindeer.

The reindeer didn't like being frightened. In an instant their speed trebled. Sleigh bells **jingling** furiously, they rocketed **higher** and **higher**, their hooves silently pounding the air. Across the sky they galloped, twisting and swerving in bursts of fear and anger. And then, suddenly, as one, they jolted and bucked. The harnesses cracked like a whip; the sleigh jerked and jackknifed.

'WOOOOOAAAAAHHHHH!!!!'

yelled the badgers, clinging on to their seats for dear life.

'AAAAAAAAAAARGH!!!!!!!'

'HEEEEEELP!!!!!!!!!'

yelled Harry the Badger, who couldn't cling on to his seat because he was clinging on to the reins.

'OH, DEAR!!!!!!'

yelled the rest of the badgers, as Harry the Badger
was flung into the air above the sleigh. The reins
snaked out, lashing like a whip.

'AAAAAAAAAAAARGH!!!!!!!!!'

Harry the Badger yelled again, as the end
of the reins slipped from his grasp and he
was flicked high into the sky.

'EEEEEEEEEKKKK!!!!!!!!!'

he continued, all four paws paddling frantically
as he turned in the air and plummeted
towards the earth.

51

'PHEWWW!!!!!!!!!!'

he went on, as the sleigh passed under him and he
managed to grab hold of the back.

'THAAAAAAANKS!!!!!!!!!'

he added, as Rolf the Badger passed him a mug of tea.

"AAAAAAAAAAAAARGHIIIIIII!"

he concluded, as the sleigh rushed on, its mad dash across the moonlit sky growing ever wilder. Below them, the little island of Great Kerfuffle flashed by.

chapter 7

In which we don't actually get back to Stinkbomb & Ketchup-Face yet

At this point, the story really should have gone back to where we left Stinkbomb and Ketch-up-Face. But instead, it decided to have one more look at the badgers; and so it moved forward to somewhere between **chapters four** and **five** . . .

Chapter 4½

In which the sleigh is still out of control

The reindeer, though still a bit frightened, were by this time mostly rather cross. They had been reindeering for Father Christmas for quite a long time, and they knew what Christmas Eve involved. It involved galloping through the sky; and **stamping** their hooves on rooftops; and being given carrots and apples. It did not involve badgers; it did not involve driving too fast; and it most definitely did not involve AAAAAAAAAAARGH!!!!!!!!!

Moreover, they could tell that Father Christmas was somewhere nearby; but they could also tell that he was not holding the reins—indeed, at this moment, no one was. Consequently, they were not sure where to go, but they were hoping that if they kept **zig-zagging** across the sky then perhaps the badgers would go away and the AAAAAAAAAAARGH!!!!!!!!!! would stop.

Father Christmas, meanwhile, was entirely fed up. He was tied up in his own sack, in the back of his own sleigh which was dashing across the sky much too quickly, and he was not enjoying the ride at all.

By this point the sleigh had hurtled, in a very uncontrolled and **zig-zaggy** sort of way, far from its starting point on the roof of the jail in the tiny village of Loose Chippings. First it had shot out to sea and raced three times round the island. Then it had turned and darted inland, and its wild and random course had taken it over—in no particular order—the Royal Palace, the tiddly little villages of Asillyname and Stupidity, the treacherous Mountains of Doom, the dreadful Swamp of Misery, the enchanted wood wherein the badgers dwell when they're not being in prison, and the proposed site of the Great Kerfuffle out-of-town rubbishmarket (a rubbishmarket is just like a supermarket except that instead of being super, it's rubbish); although it had actually stopped for a moment above the legendary **Traffic Lights of Waiting Rather a Long Time**, until the reindeer had remembered that they were flying reindeer pulling a magic sleigh, and not a bus.

Now, had they but known it, they were flashing across the sky above Stinkbomb's and Ketchup-Face's house, and heading for the Royal Palace. Apart from Harry the Badger, the badgers were quite enjoying the ride—especially now that the reindeer had started **zooming** down towards the earth and up again at the last minute, rather as if they were on an invisible rollercoaster.

'It's a bit like a doom, isn't it?' said Stewart the Badger, who thought that a doom was a kind of bouncy castle.

'Not really,' said Rolf the Badger, who didn't.

'AAAAAAAAAAAAAAAAARGH

said Harry the Badger, and took another sip of tea. 'It's going a bit cold,' he added. 'Make us another one, Rolf the Badger.

'AAAAAAAAAAAARGHIIIII...'

he added, as the sleigh plunged earthwards.

'What was that?' asked Stewart the Badger, as they shot back into the sky. 'I thought I just heard something go, *DUCK!*'

'Oh,' said Rolf the Badger. 'Maybe it was a duck.'

'I don't think ducks go *duck*,' said Stewart the Badger. 'I think they go **quack**.'

'Oh,' said Rolf the Badger, and scratched his head. 'OK. Well, if it went **quack**, it would be a duck. So I suppose if it went *duck*, it must be a **quack**.'

'*Oooh*,' said Stewart the Badger. 'I've never seen a **quack** before. I wonder what they look like.' He went to lean over the side of the sleigh, just as it plummeted earthwards once more.

59

went Harry the Badger.

'DUCK!' went the **quack**. A moment later, it added, 'NO! I MEAN ACTUALLY DUCK!!!!'

The sleigh rocketed skywards again. 'AAAAAAAAAAARGH!!!!!!!!!' Harry the Badger went, and added, 'Right, badgers, I've had more than enough of this. Come on, help me get back in.'

'OK,' said the badgers, and they all rushed to the back of the sleigh. This, of course, made the sleigh tip up; the harnesses whiplashed, flipping the reindeer towards the sky. The reindeer, panicked, galloped faster, momentum taking them higher and further round, into a great loop-the-loop in front of the moon.

'Ooooooh!!!' went the badgers.

'Come on!' Harry the Badger grumbled. 'Help me in!'

The badgers **clustered** more tightly. They **squished** and **crushed** and **squashed** against one another; they **jostled** and **elbowed** and **bundled untidily**; they **shoved** and **bumped** and **knocked** together. And with a great **heave**, they pulled Harry the Badger in.

In all the commotion, none of them noticed that as they pulled him in, they had also pushed the sack out.

Nor did they notice the story going back to Stinkbomb and Ketchup-Face, just at the point where we left them.

chapter 8

Stinkbomb shrugged. 'Dunno,' he said. 'Let's go and see the king.'

'Come on, Sacky!' said Ketchup-Face cheerily.

'Lmmmmmp mmmmmmmmp mmmmmmmmt!!!!'

went Sacky. Ketchup-Face scratched it behind where its ear would have been if it had had one,

and they began to trudge—except for Sacky, who
sighed an oddly muffled sort of sigh and began to
move with a funny sort of two-footed **hop**, leaving deep tennis racquet-shaped tracks in the snow.

Before long, they reached the Royal Palace,
which was about the size of a small cottage. It had
pretty little towers with thatched turrets, and dinky

little battlements, and the sweetest little sentry box you've ever seen. The sentry box was currently empty, because Malcolm the Cat—who was the entire army of Great Kerfuffle—wasn't there. Next to the sentry box stood a pretty little Christmas tree decorated with **shiny** baubles in the shape of dead mice, while the palace itself was bedecked with straggly **tinsel** and a few **fairy lights**.

Stinkbomb raised his hand to the door and knocked.

A window opened above them, and King Toothbrush Weasel leaned out. He was holding a candle in a little sort of saucery candle-holder with a handle, like you so often see in Christmas stories, and wearing a nightcap and a yellow checked dressing gown to which was pinned a badge that said (Night Porter). 'Yes?' he called, a little grumpily.

'Happy Christmas, King Toothbrush Weasel!'

Ketchup-Face called out.

'Except it isn't,' added Stinkbomb. 'Happy, that is.'

King Toothbrush Weasel looked stern. 'I am not King Toothbrush Weasel,' he said, tapping his badge. 'I am the night porter. What do you want?'

'Oh, *please* be King Toothbrush Weasel,' said Ketchup-Face. 'It's important.'

'Or, at least,' added Stinkbomb, 'could you get him for us, please? It's an emergency!'

King Toothbrush Weasel continued to look stern. 'His Royal Highness King Toothbrush Weasel is fast asleep in bed, waiting for Father Christmas to bring him his presents,' he said.

'But there won't be any presents!'

Ketchup-Face protested.

'Father Christmas has disappeared,' added Stinkbomb.

'Ah,' said King Toothbrush Weasel. 'Well, that *does* sound like an emergency. Wait there—I shall wake King Toothbrush Weasel.'

'You'd better tell him to get dressed,' Stink-bomb added.

'Yes,' agreed Ketchup-Face. ''Cos we're in a story, and he doesn't like being in a story in his dressing gown.'

King Toothbrush Weasel went a bit red, and pulled his dressing gown tighter around himself. 'I shall tell him,' he said, and disappeared inside the palace, shutting the window behind him.

Stinkbomb and Ketchup-Face waited.

The window opened again.

'What on *earth* have you got with you?' King Toothbrush Weasel asked.

Ketchup-Face grinned, showing the place where she had recently lost a tooth. 'That's Sacky,' she said. 'She's my new pet. Isn't she *lovely*?'

'Hmmmmmp!'

went Sacky.

'Lmmmp mmmmmm mmmmmmmmmt!!!'

'How extraordinary!' said King Toothbrush Weasel. 'I wonder what sort of animal she is? I expect King Toothbrush Weasel will know. He's an expert on animals.'

And he closed the window again.

Once more, Stinkbomb and Ketchup-Face waited.

'Stinkbomb?' Ketchup-Face said.

'Yes?' said Stinkbomb.

'Where are we going after we've talked to King Toothbrush Weasel?'

Stinkbomb scratched his head. 'I don't know,' he said.

'Oh,' said Ketchup-Face. 'I bet Miss Butterworth would know. I wish she was here.'

'I am here,' said Miss Butterworth, in a voice like the sound of tinkling wind-chimes.

69

'Ow!' said a small heap of snow, and Malcolm the Cat exploded from it.

'Oh, sorry,' said Miss Butterworth, looking down into the snow and taking her foot off Malcolm the Cat's tail. Malcolm the Cat looked grumpily at her and crawled off to sleep in the sentry box.

Miss Butterworth was a member of the Ancient Order of Ninja Librarians. She was tall and thin, and normally dressed in black clothing of fine silk; but tonight she was dressed in white. *'I am on night manoeuvres,'* she said. *'I have an urgent mission to carry out.'*

'Oooh!' said Stinkbomb excitedly. 'Are you chasing baddies and chopping their heads off with your big sword?'

'No,' said Miss Butterworth. *'I am slipping into people's houses and taking their overdue library books back before Christmas Day.'*

'Isn't that against the law?' Ketchup-Face asked.

'Not for a Ninja Librarian,' Miss Butterworth said. *'Besides, if they have too many overdue library*

books, they might end up on Father Christmas's Naughty List. So, really, I am doing them a favour.'

'Talking of Father Christmas,' Stinkbomb began; but just at that moment, the door of the palace opened, and King Toothbrush Weasel appeared. He had dressed himself in his most regal snowsuit, to which he had pinned a badge that said ⟨King⟩. He had also put on his red velvet robe trimmed with pretend fur, a special Christmas beard with **twinkly lights** and **tinsel** in it, a small crown—which looked slightly odd, since he'd forgotten to take off his nightcap—and a pair of wellies.

'Ah, Stinkbomb and Ketchup-Face,' he began. 'Glumph!!!!!' he added, disappearing into the deep snow outside the palace door.

Stinkbomb and Ketchup-Face helped him out and tied tennis racquets to his feet.

'Now,' said King Toothbrush Weasel, 'tell me all about this disappearing Father Christmas.'

'Well,' said Ketchup-Face, 'it's Father Christmas.'

'He's disappeared,' said Stinkbomb.

'And we don't know where he is,' Ketchup-Face continued.

'Mmmmm hmmmmm!!!!! Mmmmmm hmmmmmmmm!!!!!'

went Sacky.

'That's an interesting pet,' said King Tooth-brush Weasel. 'I thought I knew about every kind of animal, but I've never seen one of those.'

'Her name's Sacky,' said Ketchup-Face proudly. 'I found her and she's mine.'

'Mmmmmmm nmmmmmmmt Smmmmmmmm!!!'

went Sacky.

'Mmmmmm Fmmmm mmmmm Crmmmmmsmmmms!!!'

'Maybe it's hungry,' suggested Stinkbomb.

'Oh,' said Ketchup-Face. 'But she hasn't got a mouth.'

'It can't be that, then,' said Stinkbomb. 'Anyway, we really ought to find Father Christmas. Has anyone got any ideas?'

Sacky sighed its funny muffled sort of sigh again.

74

'Miss Butterworth might,' said Ketchup-Face.

'But where is she?' asked Stinkbomb; and they realized that, as silently as she had come, Miss Butterworth had vanished.

'Oh, dear,' said King Toothbrush Weasel. 'Well, perhaps the army will have an idea.'

The army, curled up on top of his tall, black, furry guardsman's hat, gave a **loud snore**.

'It doesn't look like it,' said Stinkbomb. 'Maybe we should look for clues.'

'Good idea,' said King Toothbrush Weasel. 'What about his pythons? Has anyone seen them?'

'What pythons?' asked Ketchup-Face.

'Oh, *you* know,' said King Toothbrush Weasel. 'Father Christmas's sleigh is pulled through the sky by eight flying pythons.'

'Um . . . reindeer,' said Stinkbomb politely.

'It's rude to call a king "dear,"' said King Tooth-brush Weasel. 'You should call me "Your Majesty." And it's not rain, it's snow,' he continued.

'No, you silly king,' said Ketchup-Face. 'He means Father Christmas's sleigh is pulled by flying reindeer.'

'Don't be ridiculous,' said King Toothbrush Weasel. '*All* reindeer fly. But eight of them wouldn't be strong enough to pull a sleigh. You'd need thousands. And he'd never get all the way round the world if his sleigh was pulled by reindeer; they'd keep stopping to bash into lightbulbs . . . '

'I think you're thinking of moths, Your Majesty,' Stinkbomb said. 'Anyway, we really ought to try to find Father Christmas.'

'I bet Miss Butterworth could help,' said Ketchup-Face. 'I wonder where she went?'

'I am here,' Miss Butterworth said again, appearing in the palace doorway. She was holding a large pile of books, which bore titles such as *The One-Minute King* and *Who Moved My Throne?* and *Reigning for Dummies*.

'Oh,' said King Toothbrush Weasel, going red again. 'Are those overdue already? My, how time flies . . . '

'Miss Butterworth,' said Ketchup-Face, 'can you tell us anything that might guide us on our quest?'

Miss Butterworth nodded wisely. *'Help will arrive,'* she said, *'when you most need it.'*

'Oooh,' said Stinkbomb, impressed. 'Did you find that out by tapping into some mystical force?'

'No,' said Miss Butterworth. *'But I've noticed that that's what normally happens in these stories.'* Then her eyes crinkled as if, behind the white scarf

that covered her face, a wide smile had spread across her face. *'Merry Christmas. And for now, farewell.'*

'Miss Butterworth! Wait!' said Ketchup-Face.

'Father Christmas is missing!'

'Mmmmmm mmmmmm Fmmmmmmmmm Crmmmmmsmmmms!!!'

said Sacky.

But Miss Butterworth was no longer there.

'How *does* she do that?' said King Toothbrush Weasel.

'I think it's ninja librarian magic,' said Ketch-up-Face solemnly.

'I used to think that,' said Stinkbomb. 'But I wonder if it might be some sort of camouflage. That might explain why she was dressed in white instead of her usual black. Oh, sorry,' he added, stepping to one side as a mound of snow crept past him. He paused, thinking. 'Actually, no. It's probably magic.'

'Anyway,' Ketchup-Face said.

'Come on! We're having an adventure! We have to rescue Father Christmas! Let's go!'

'Go where?' asked King Toothbrush Weasel.

'Well,' said Stinkbomb, scratching his head, 'we haven't been to Loose Chippings yet. We usually go there at least once every story.'

'Excellent suggestion!' said King Toothbrush Weasel. 'Loose Chippings it is!'

'Right!' agreed Stinkbomb. 'Let's go! Come *on*, Ketchup-Face!!!' This last was said slightly tetchily as, despite her enthusiasm for the adventure, Ketchup-

Face had just taken one of her snowshoes off and was having a game of tennis with an owl. The owl had rolled itself up into a ball and was going 'Wheeee!' as Ketchup-Face hit it over the fence.

'Awww,' said the owl, as Ketchup-Face sat down and put the snowshoe back on.

'Sorry, owl,' said Stinkbomb, helping her with the straps. 'We've got to get to Loose Chippings as quickly as possible. And it'll take us *ages* to get there in the snow.'

But just then, there was a **swishing** sound, and a very welcome figure appeared, gliding past the palace garden.

'Starlight! My horsey!' exclaimed Ketch-up-Face, delighted to see their friend the little shopping trolley, who was not a horsey and was not called Starlight.

The little shopping trolley **skidded** to a halt. It looked a little guilty, which was odd for two reasons—firstly because, in all the time that

Stinkbomb and Ketchup-Face had known it, it had never been anything but good and kind and honest; and secondly because, being a little shopping trolley, it didn't have a face.

'Oh . . . hello,' said the little shopping trolley. 'Er . . . what are you doing out of bed? Shouldn't you be asleep, so that Father Christmas will bring you presents?'

'We're having an adventure,' Stinkbomb said. 'What are *you* doing out of bed?'

'Er . . . I'm on my way to . . . um . . . somewhere,' said the little shopping trolley evasively.

'Never mind that now!' said King Toothbrush Weasel. 'We have an emergency to unemergence!'

'OK' said the little shopping trolley. 'Er . . . well . . . bye, then.'

'No!' said Stinkbomb. 'Don't go! We need your help!'

'Oh,' said the shopping trolley, looking strangely unwilling.

'Do we?' said King Toothbrush Weasel.

'Yes, of course we do!' said Stinkbomb. 'The little shopping trolley can carry us much faster than we can walk in these snowshoes!'

'Wouldn't its wheels get stuck in the snow?' King Toothbrush Weasel asked puzzledly.

'Good point,' said Stinkbomb. 'Except they weren't, were they?'

'No, they weren't,' said Ketchup-Face. 'How did you do that **swishy** thing just now? Horsies don't go **swish!**'

'I'm not a horsey,' the little shopping trolley said, turning and reluctantly **swishing** in through the gate.

And now, of course, they could all see that it was gliding on skis.

'Excellent!' said King Toothbrush Weasel, taking a sticker out of his pocket, writing the words Royal Sleigh on it, and sticking it to the little shopping trolley's handlebar. Encumbered by snowshoes, he, Stinkbomb, and Ketchup-Face scrambled into its basket and pulled Sacky in after them. 'To Loose Chippings!' he added in his kingliest voice.

'Oh,' said the little shopping trolley. 'Er . . . you're sure you wouldn't rather go somewhere else?'

'Quite sure,' said King Toothbrush Weasel. 'Come on!'

'Really?' said the little shopping trolley.

'Really,' said King Toothbrush Weasel.

'I hear Asillyname's nice at this time of year,' said the little shopping trolley.

'I don't want to go to Asillyname,' said King Toothbrush Weasel sharply. 'I want to go to Loose Chippings.'

'What about Stupidity?' the little shopping trolley suggested. 'I've always wanted to go to Stupidity.'

'Come on, Starlight, giddy up!' Ketchup-Face put in. 'We *have* to go to Loose Chippings'

'We could go for a nice ride along the river,' said the little shopping trolley. 'Or into the woods?'

'This is getting ridiculous,' King Toothbrush Weasel complained. 'Royal Sleigh, I command you to take us to Loose Chippings! At once! With no more arguing! Or suffer my royal displeasure!'

'Oh,' said the little shopping trolley. 'Er . . . all right, then.'

And with great reluctance, it turned and swished out of the gate again.

'This isn't the way to Loose Chippings!' Stink-bomb said after a moment.

'Isn't it?' said the little shopping trolley. 'Are you sure?'

'**YES!!!**₀₀₀' said Stinkbomb, Ketchup-Face, and King Toothbrush Weasel together.

'It . . . er . . . it might be a different way to Loose Chippings. Shall we keep going for a bit, and see?' said the little shopping trolley, not slowing down even a bit.

'**NO!!!**₀₀₀'

said Stinkbomb, Ketchup-Face, and King Tooth-brush Weasel together.

'Oh,' said the little shopping trolley. 'Well . . . OK then. I'll just look for a sensible place to turn round.'

'What's wrong with right here?' asked Stink-bomb. 'Honestly, anyone would think you didn't want to take us to Loose Chippings.'

The little shopping trolley said nothing, but turned unwillingly around.

chapter 11

In which our heroes reach Loose Chippings,
and a secret is revealed

Imagine a sleigh-ride across a snowy landscape at dead of night on Christmas Eve. Imagine the bright clear moon shining down, and the stars

twinkling like faraway candles. Imagine the cold crispness of winter against your cheeks, and your breath curling like mist in the frosty air.

And then imagine that there is a king grumbling behind you; and a boy **wriggling** around so that his snowshoes stick into your bottom; and a girl singing the words *Jingle Bells* over and over again at the top of her voice, pausing only to shout, 'Giddy-up, Starlight!'; and a creature like a sack with a pair of boots sticking out going, `Lmmmm mmmmm mmmmmt!'. And imagine that the sleigh doesn't actually want to go where it's going. And imagine that it's not really a sleigh, but a little shopping trolley wearing a pair of skis.

The journey was more or less like that.

It was not far, and soon the village lay below them. But unexpectedly, in Loose Chippings the night was neither silent nor still. They could make out tiny flickering lights gliding eerily through the streets, and hear mysterious music such as they had never heard before.

'Whatever is going on down there?' said King Toothbrush Weasel in puzzlement.

'Er . . . maybe it's not safe,' said the little shopping trolley, sliding to a stop on the hillside. 'Let's go somewhere else instead.'

'No!' said Ketchup-Face defiantly.

'Whatever's going on down there, our mission is to solve the mystery and find Father Christmas!'

'Mmmmm mmmmm Fmmmm-mmmmm Crmmmmms-mmmms!' said Sacky.

'Oh, yes,' added Ketchup-Face, patting Sacky on what she guessed might be its head. 'And take good care of Sacky. That's very important.'

'Yes!' agreed Stinkbomb. 'And we will carry out our mission even if it means dying a horrible death or something!'

'Oh,' said King Toothbrush Weasel. 'Oh. Do you think that's very likely? Perhaps we shouldn't go to Loose Chippings after all.'

'Good idea!' said the little shopping trolley, turning round enthusiastically.

'NO!!!!!' said Stinkbomb and Ketchup-Face together.

The little shopping trolley stopped, mid-turn.

'Why don't you want us to go to Loose Chippings?' Stinkbomb asked.

'Yes,' agreed Ketchup-Face. 'You're being a very silly horsey.'

'Well . . . er . . . it's just that . . . ' the little shopping trolley began. But it got no further, for suddenly all around them the snow erupted like a circle of icy volcanoes, and from its depths appeared creatures so terrifying that quite unexpectedly the **chapter** came to an end.

chapter 12

In which some terrifying creatures turn out to be slightly less terrifying than expected, but still a bit scary

'Wuurrrgh!!!' roared the terrifying creatures. 'Urrrgh! Wurrrrgh!'

The little shopping trolley trembled so hard that its basket **rattled**; and the basket's occupants shrank away from the terrifying creatures and huddled together for reassurance.

'Wh-what are they?' asked Ketchup-Face nervously.

'Terrifying creatures, I think,' said Stinkbomb.

'Nonsense,' said King Toothbrush Weasel. 'These creatures are terrifying, and terrifying creatures aren't. Oh . . . Wait a minute . . .'

'Mmmmmt mmm mmmmmmth mms mmmmng mmmn?'

said Sacky.

The hideous, monstrous faces of the terrifying creatures leered horribly at them. One had long, sharp fangs; another had twisted, demonic horns; a third had a single enormous bloodshot eye in the middle of its forehead. No two were alike. All they had in common was this: firstly, each terrifying creature's face was terrifying; and secondly, each terrifying creature's face was tied to its basket with string.

'Hang on,' said Stinkbomb. 'Baskets? String?'

'Oh! Yes!' said Ketchup-Face. 'And they've got wheels, too! Look!'

It was true: each of the terrifying creatures had little wheels beneath its wiry basket; and all had skis fixed to the wheels, except for one who had tennis racquets tied on with bits of string.

'Wait a minute,' said Stinkbomb. 'You're just shopping trolleys wearing masks!'

'Of course we are!' said one of the shopping trolleys. 'What else would we be?'

'We had you fooled, though, didn't we!' said another.

'Well, yes, you did,' said Stinkbomb, breathing a sigh of relief. 'We thought we were in trouble there.'

'Well,' said one of the shopping trolleys, 'obviously, you are. An awful lot of trouble. You've probably never been in such serious trouble in your whole life. I might go so far as to say that you have doomed yourselves.'

'It was funny, though, wasn't it?' added the shopping trolley with the tennis racquets hopefully.

The little shopping trolley began to tremble violently. 'Oh, dear,' it said. 'This is all my fault.'

'Is it?' said the shopping trolley whose mask had twisted demonic horns. 'Oh. Well, I suppose you've probably doomed *your*self, too. Come on.'

And without further ado, the shopping trolleys began to shepherd them down the hill towards the dark and snow-covered village.

'Stop, you naughties!' said Ketchup-Face crossly. 'We don't want to be bullied and pushed around!'

'You've no one to blame but yourselves, I'm afraid,' said the shopping trolley with the fanged mask. 'You have trespassed on the most sacred and secret night in the shopping trolleys' calendar.'

'Actually, it's the *only* sacred and secret night in the shopping trolleys' calendar,' pointed out one of the others.

'Oh, yes. Good point,' said the other. 'Anyway, you have trespassed upon the festival of . . . TrolleyHoliday™!'

The other shopping trolleys all made spooky noises.

'Mmmmmts nmmmt Mmmmm-mmm-Mmm-mmm-mmm! Mmmmts Crmmmmms-mmmms Mmmmv!'

said Sacky.

Ketchup-Face gave it a reassuring pat. 'It's not TrolleyHoliday™' she said. 'It's Christmas Eve.'

'Mmmmmmts mmmmmm Mmmm mmmmmd!'

said Sacky.

'Er . . . not for shopping trolleys,' said the little shopping trolley. 'While you're having Christmas Eve, shopping trolleys have TrolleyHoliday™. It's a celebration of the fact that all the supermarkets are closed the next day and we get the day off, so we can stay up late and have fun.'

'And now,' the shopping trolley continued, 'we must take you to the Queen of TrolleyHoliday™, who will decide your fate!'

Already they had reached the bottom of the hill. Now they could see that Loose Chippings was filled with shopping trolleys, wearing terrifying masks and gliding on skis; the lights they had seen from the hillside were torches that the trolleys held in their baskets. From all around them came the eerie music they had heard; but as they came to a stop in the village square, the shopping trolleys who had been singing their TrolleyHoliday™ hymn fell silent as they saw the trespassers in their midst. They gathered round until the little shopping trolley was entirely surrounded.

And then the crowd parted, and a shopping trolley wearing a particularly hideous mask and a golden crown glided forwards.

'So,' it said threateningly. 'What have we here?'

'Trespassers, your majesty,' said the shopping trolley with the horned mask. 'Brought here by this traitor to trolley-kind!'

'He's not a traitor to trolley-kind!'

shouted Ketchup-Face bravely, and then spoiled the effect a bit by adding, 'He's a beautiful horsey called Starlight!'

'I'm not a horsey,' said the little shopping trolley. 'And I'm not a traitor, either,' it added quietly.

'No?' said the Queen of TrolleyHoliday™. 'Then what are these humans doing in your basket, spying upon us on this night of all nights?'

'We're trying to rescue Father Christmas, actually,' said Stinkbomb.

'Mmmmm mmmmm Fmmmm-mmmmm Crmmmmms-mmmmms!'

said Sacky.

'They're certainly not spying,' said the little shopping trolley.

'A likely story!' said the Queen. 'You've been a very naughty trolley, Olivia!'

'Olivia?' said Stinkbomb. 'Didn't you once tell us your name was Eric?'

'Oh,' explained the little shopping trolley, 'it was. But that was because I was a bit wet, and I'd just met you.'

'Eh?' said Stinkbomb, puzzled.

'All shopping trolleys are called Louise,' explained the little shopping trolley, 'but only the first time you meet them, and only if they're completely dry. If they're wet, then they're called Eric, unless it's just the handle that's wet, in which case they're called Beyoncé.'

'But the Queen just called you Olivia!' said Ketchup-Face.

'That's because it's TrolleyHoliday™ and there's snow on the ground,' the little shopping trolley said patiently.

'And what would you be called if it was TrolleyHoliday™ but there wasn't snow on the ground?' asked King Toothbrush Weasel.

'Ahmed, of course,' said the little shopping trolley. 'Unless it was a Tuesday.'

'Well,' the Queen said, 'now your name is . . . Archibald!'

'Ooooh!' said all the other shopping trolleys excitedly.

The little shopping trolley began to shake.

'Er . . . what does it mean if you're called Archibald?' Stinkbomb asked, not sure that he would like the answer.

'It means,' growled the Queen of Trolley Holiday™, 'that you and all your contents are about to suffer a dreadful punishment!'

Chapter 13

In which the little shopping trolley and all its contents suffer a dreadful punishment

'**Wuurrrgh!!!**' roared the shopping trolleys, rattling their wheels fearfully. 'The dreadful punishment!'

'Starlight,' said Ketchup-Face quietly, 'what *is* the dreadful punishment?'

'I don't know,' said the little shopping trolley. 'And my name's not Starlight. It's Olivia. I mean, it's Archibald. Oh dear.'

'Are you ready to meet your **doom**?' asked the Queen of TrolleyHoliday™.

Stinkbomb thought about this. The idea of meeting his **doom** certainly sounded interesting, but on balance he wasn't sure if he fancied it.

'Er . . . no,' he said.

'Tough!' the Queen answered. 'Take them to the skiing area!'

'The skiing area!!!!' yelled all the other shopping trolleys, and they herded the little shopping trolley, with Stinkbomb, Ketchup-Face, King Toothbrush Weasel, and Sacky inside it, to the middle of the village square, which was—as always at this time of year—decorated with a lovely Christmas tree which stood nearly a metre tall, strung with as many as **three fairy lights**. Great Kerfuffle was not a wealthy kingdom.

Stinkbomb and Ketchup-Face gasped, for in the centre of the square, right next to the tree, the shopping trolleys had made the **biggest** mound of snow they had ever seen. It rose **up** like a small mountain, towering over them.

'Now,' said the Queen of TrolleyHoliday™. 'Prepare to face your dreadful punishment!'

'What are you going to do to us?' demanded Ketchup-Face bravely.

'We're going to take you **up** to the top,' said the Queen of TrolleyHoliday™, 'and make you slide all the way down!'

Stinkbomb and Ketchup-Face looked at one another.

'Er . . . that doesn't sound very dreadful,' said Stinkbomb.

The Queen glided menacingly towards them. 'It will be,' she hissed. She turned to her followers and in a terrible voice she commanded:

'Take them to the top, and give them a bit of a push!'

Immediately, the crowd parted around the little shopping trolley, and the trolleys who had first captured them began to push it **up** the enormous mound of snow.

'What *is* going on?' asked King Toothbrush Weasel.

'Um . . . I'm not sure,' whispered the little shopping trolley. 'It really doesn't seem like a very dreadful punishment.'

'No,' agreed Stinkbomb. 'But I think we ought to play along with it, just in case they think of something worse.'

From the top, the mound of snow looked even taller. They looked down the steep slope to the crowd of hideously masked shopping trolleys below them.

'Push them! Push them!'

shouted one of the trolleys.

'Give them a bit of a shove!' shouted another.

'Wurrrrgh!' said several more, just to be scary.

And suddenly, they felt a bit of a push from behind. Then they were rushing down the mound of snow, with the cold air lashing at their faces.

'Wheeeeeeeee!' yelled Ketchup-Face. 'Oh . . . er . . . I mean . . . help?'

'Um, yes,' agreed Stinkbomb. 'Someone save us from this terrible danger. If it's not too much trouble.'

Moments later, they had reached the bottom of the slope and were gliding to a stop just next to the Queen.

'Again! Again!' shouted Ketchup-Face happily. 'Er . . . I mean . . . Please don't do that dreadful punishment to us again! Again!'

'Good idea,' said the Queen. 'Punish them again!'

'Oh, no,' said Stinkbomb. 'Never have I been punished so dreadfully. It was really dreadful. And, er, punishy.'

'Wurrrgh!' yelled the other shopping trolleys happily, rattling their wheels.

The Queen raised her voice once more. 'Take them to the top of the mound once more!'

'Do you have to?' Stinkbomb asked. 'It was great fun—I mean, it was a dreadful punishment, and everything, but we do have a mission to get on with.'

'Tough,' said the Queen.

'Yeah,' said one of the other shopping trolleys. 'We're going to make this story more exciting if it takes us till . . . er . . . the end of the story!'

'Shhhh!' hissed the Queen, but too late.

Stinkbomb and Ketchup-Face looked at one another in puzzlement.

'What do you mean?' asked Ketchup-Face.

The Queen sighed. 'If you must know,' she said, 'we're not really bad guys. We just wanted to give the story a bit of extra **oomph**. You know, seeing as there don't seem to be any badgers around.'

'You mean you're just pretending to be scary to make the story more exciting?' asked Ketchup-Face. 'And TrolleyHoliday™ isn't real?'

'It's real, all right!' said the Queen. 'We put on scary masks and jump out at each other, and sing spooky songs, and have jelly and ice cream. It's great fun. It's just not terribly sacred or secret. We're not really that bothered about people finding out about it, if I'm honest.'

'Aren't we?' said the little shopping trolley in great surprise.

'No, not at all,' said the Queen. 'That's just something we tell the younger shopping trolleys because . . . er . . . well, I'm not sure why, really. I suppose it's just the sort of thing grown-ups tell children.'

'Oh,' said Stinkbomb. 'But we need to get on with our quest.'

'Well, you can't,' said the Queen. 'We may not really be bad guys, but we're going to go on menacing you excitingly until some proper bad guys show up!'

But just at that moment, the moonlight was blotted out. A sound came from above them—a horrible, unearthly sound, like the screaming of a load of badgers in an out-of-control magic sleigh—and they looked up to see something large hurtling out of the night towards them.

Chapter 14

In which the quest appears to be over

'Look out!' yelled Ketchup-Face.

'OK!' said the shopping trolleys, and they all looked out.

'Duck!' shouted Stinkbomb.

'Oh, no,' said the Queen of TrolleyHoliday™. 'It's much too big to be a duck.'

'GET OUT OF THE WAY!!!!'

bellowed Stinkbomb and Ketchup-Face together, leaping out of the little shopping trolley and running for cover; and the shopping trolleys all got out of the way, just as the thing—whatever it was—plummeted from the sky and drove itself deep into the towering mound of snow.

The shopping trolleys panicked.

they yelled. 'Unexpected item in the skiing area!' And they fled in every direction.

Suddenly, the village square was deserted except for Stinkbomb and Ketchup-Face, for the little shopping trolley—with King Toothbrush Weasel and Sacky inside—had taken refuge behind the library. They looked at the mound of snow. There was a great hole in it now, from which protruded something that looked very much like the back of a sleigh; and from deep inside the hole there came a number of **groaning** sounds. Stinkbomb really felt that there should have been wisps of smoke trailing from the hole; but there weren't.

Cautiously, Stinkbomb and Ketchup-Face approached, and peered inside.

'Um . . . hello?' Stinkbomb called.

The **groaning** sounds stopped. There was a **muttering**; and then a **scuffling**. Stinkbomb and Ketchup-Face stepped back, as a large number of figures emerged from the hole and clambered out, dusting themselves down.

'Who are you?' asked Ketchup-Face.

'Isn't it obvious?' answered one of the figures. 'We're Father Christmas and all his elves and reindeer.'

'Really?' said Stinkbomb. 'Are you *sure* you're Father Christmas and all his elves and reindeer?'

'Oh, yes,' said the figure. 'We're definitely Father Christmas and all his elves and reindeer. We're very Father-Christmas-and-all-his-elves-and-reindeery indeed. Isn't that right, Rolf the Red-Nosed Reindeer?'

'That's right,' agreed Rolf the Red-Nosed Reindeer, a big red-nosed reindeer with a big badge that said $\left(\text{Red-Nosed}\atop\text{Reindeer}\right)$. 'We're Father Christmas and all his elves and reindeer all right. Aren't we, Harry the Father Christmas?'

'Yes,' agreed Harry the Father Christmas, taking a sip of tea from a mug marked, [World's Best Father Christmas]. 'We're extremely Father-Christmas-and-all-his-elves-and-reindeery. Aren't we, Stewart the Elf?'

Just as Stewart the Elf was opening his mouth to answer, Harry the Father Christmas passed him a note that said:

> Pretend we're Father Christmas and all his elves and reindeer.

Stewart the Elf read it slowly three times and then said, 'Er, we're Father Christmas and all his elves and reindeer.'

He turned the note over. On the other side it said:

> Don't let them know we're badgers.

'Er, we're not badgers,' he added.

'Oh, OK,' said Ketchup-Face. 'Then our quest is over! We've been looking for you!'

'Well, you're not *supposed* to be looking for us!' said Harry the Father Christmas. 'Don't you know that you don't get any **presents** if you see Father Christmas on the night of Christmas Eve?'

'Oh!' said both Stinkbomb and Ketchup-Face, remembering, and they shut their eyes.

'Har har har,' laughed Harry the Father Christmas. 'Er . . . I mean, ho ho ho. Now, just keep your eyes closed for a few minutes while we scarper. I mean, while we, um, find your presents in the back of the sleigh.'

Stinkbomb and Ketchup-Face waited with their eyes closed. There was a noise that sounded like a lot of presents being dragged from a sleigh; and a noise that sounded like a snowmobile's engine being started up; and another noise that sounded like **scarpering**.

Stinkbomb and Ketchup-Face waited a bit more.

And then a voice spoke.

Chapter 15

In which Stinkbomb and Ketchup-Face stop waiting, and some other things happen

'Why on earth are you standing there with your eyes closed?' asked the voice. It sounded rather like King Toothbrush Weasel.

'So that Father Christmas will bring us our presents,' explained Stinkbomb.

'Mmmmm mmmmm Fmmmm-mmmmm Crmmmmms-mmmms!'

said another voice, which sounded rather like Sacky.

'Close your eyes, Sacky!' said Ketchup-Face. 'Father Christmas won't bring you anything if you see him!'

'But we can't see Father Christmas anyway,' said a third voice, which sounded very much like the little shopping trolley. 'I don't think he's here.'

'Oh,' said Stinkbomb and Ketchup-Face together, opening their eyes.

'He was here a minute ago,' added Ketch-up-Face.

'I wonder where he went?' said Stinkbomb. 'And, look! He's left his sleigh behind!'

Sure enough, the back of the sleigh was still sticking out of the hole. And as they looked, it moved, rather as if something was trying to pull it deeper inside.

'How strange!' said King Toothbrush Weasel.

'If it goes much further into the mound,' Stink-bomb observed, 'it might come out the other side.'

Ketchup-Face went round the other side of the mound to have a look. 'Oh!' she exclaimed in delight. 'There's a little tree growing round here!'

Stinkbomb came to see. 'So there is,' he said. 'And look! It's **wriggling!**'

'It must be a special **wriggling** tree,' Ketch-up-Face said. 'And look! There's another one!'

A second tree was indeed pushing its way out of the snow next to the first.

'Sacky! Starlight! King Toothbrush Weasel!' Ketchup-Face called. 'Come and look at the trees growing!'

'Er . . . I'm not sure that they *are* trees,' said the little shopping trolley. 'Look! They've got eyes at the bottom!'

And now everyone could see that the **wriggly** little trees were standing on small brown domes, which did indeed have eyes—large, friendly eyes that shone a warm brown in the moonlight.

The eyes blinked, and the trees **wriggled**, and suddenly Stinkbomb and Ketchup-Face and their friends were showered with snow.

'Glumph!' they all said, wiping their faces and blinking the snow out of their eyes. And when they could see again, they all gasped for there, struggling out of the snow, were the heads and necks and strong shoulders of two magnificent animals.

'Pythons!' said King Toothbrush Weasel in awe.

'Um, I think you mean reindeer, Your Majesty,' said Stinkbomb.

`Mmmmmm!
Mmmmmmmm!'

said Sacky; and at the sound of its voice the reindeer redoubled their efforts. With a great heave,
they lurched forward, and the mound of snow
collapsed with a **flumph!** The reindeer struggled free. Father Christmas's sleigh, large and sleek
and magnificent, stood there, the snow from the
collapsed mound cascading off it like a waterfall.

And then there was a **chomping** sound, and
they turned to see Sacky lying in the snow with a
reindeer nibbling at its ankles.

`Naughty reindeer!
Don't eat Sacky!'

Ketchup-Face gasped in alarm, leaping forward to help her pet. But before she reached it, the reindeer arched its neck and spat out a piece of rope, and something strange happened to Sacky.

It **wriggled**,

and **flopped**, and,

like a **snake**,

began to shed its **skin**.

Its strange sack-like covering **wrinkled**,

and **bunched** up,

and **suddenly** it was no longer Sacky lying there,

but . . .

127

'Fat
Christ

her mas!"

said Stinkbomb and Ketchup-Face, shutting their eyes tight.

Father Christmas sat up, and pulled several pieces of wrapping paper out of his mouth. 'Open your eyes, you two!' he said. 'Come on, we've got work to do!'

'But if we see you, you won't give us our presents,' said Ketchup-Face worriedly.

'Oh, yes I will,' said Father Christmas. 'You needn't worry about that.'

'But if you're Father Christmas' said Ketchup-Face, opening her eyes again, 'and these are your reindeer . . . who were all those other Father-Christmas-and-all-his-elves-and-reindeer?'

'Can't you guess?' said Father Christmas, rising and brushing himself down.

'Oh,' said Stinkbomb. 'It wasn't the badgers, was it?'

'Yes, it was,' said Father Christmas. 'And we've only got one **chapter** left in which to thwart them. Come on!'

Chapter 16

In which there is an exciting chase and the badgers are thwarted

Moments later, Stinkbomb and Ketchup-Face were scrambling excitedly into the sleigh next to Father Christmas.

'Aren't you coming?' asked Stinkbomb.

'Er, no,' said King Toothbrush Weasel. 'I'm a bit afraid of flying.'

'And I think I might be more help down on the ground!' added the little shopping trolley. 'Good luck!'

'Then a Merry Christmas to you both!' said Father Christmas, taking off the handbrake, and the reindeer stamped their feet and galloped into the sky.

'This is even better than Starlight!' said Ketchup-Face excitedly, adding, 'Don't tell him that, though. I wouldn't want to hurt his feelings.'

'Now,' said Father Christmas, 'I wonder which way they went? It looks to me as if they took the snowmobile I keep for emergencies, so look out for tracks.'

'What—like those?' said Stinkbomb, pointing at some long thin tracks in the snow.

'Exactly like those!' said Father Christmas delightedly, turning the sleigh.

It wasn't long before Ketchup-Face's sharp eyes spotted something.

'Look!' she said. 'A tall **wobbly** tree skiing into the distance!'

'That's not a **wobbly** tree!' said Stinkbomb.

'That's a tower of **badgers** on a snowmobile!'

'On, Dasher! On, Dancer! On, Prancer! On, Vixen!' said Father Christmas.

* * *

Down below, Harry the Badger looked up.

'Bother!' he said. 'They're after us! On, Rolf the Badger! On, Stewart the Badger! On, all the other badgers who we've never bothered giving names to!'

But Rolf the Badger and Stewart the Badger and all the other badgers just went on standing on each other because they thought that was what Harry the Badger meant by 'On!'

'Bother!' said Harry the Badger again. 'They're gaining on us! Quick, Rolf the Badger! You take over the controls while I keep a look out! Head for the forest!'

* * *

'They're turning!' said Ketchup-Face. 'Look! They're heading for the forest!'

'We'll lose them if they go in there!' said Stinkbomb. 'Oh. They've gone in there. What do we do now?'

'Don't give up hope yet!' said Father Christmas. 'Look!'

Stinkbomb and Ketchup-Face turned, and looked, and then they cheered; for there, below them, was their friend the little shopping trolley, with all the other shopping trolleys following on, their wire baskets gleaming heroically in the moonlight. They flashed across the snow, skiing fast and true, and disappeared into the trees.

❄   ❄   ❄

In the forest, Rolf the Badger brought the snowmobile to a halt. 'They'll never find us in here!' he said, adding, ⸢Hur hur hur!⸣ because that was his favourite **evil** laugh.

'Never!' agreed Harry the Badger, adding, 'Har, har har!' because that was his favourite **evil** laugh.

'Never ever!' agreed Stewart the Badger, adding, 'Oink, oink, oink!' because he still hadn't got the hang of the whole **evil** laugh business.

'Never ever ever!' agreed all the other badgers, adding, 'AAAAAAAAARGH!!!' because suddenly they were surrounded by a host of terrifying creatures whose hideous, monstrous faces were tied to their baskets with string.

'AAAAAAAAAARGH!!!'

agreed Rolf the Badger, Stewart the Badger,
and Harry the Badger.

'Wuurrrgh!!!...'

roared the terrifying creatures terrifyingly.

Panicking, Rolf the Badger rammed the snow-mobile into gear and the tower of badgers shot out of the forest again.

❋   ❋   ❋

'There they are!' shouted Stinkbomb. 'After them!'

'On, Comet! On, Cupid! On, Donder and Blitzen!' cried Father Christmas.

'On, Starlight!' shouted Ketchup-Face. In her excitement, she'd forgotten just for a moment that she wasn't in a little shopping trolley, but was in fact in Father Christmas's sleigh. Then she remembered, and yelled, 'Giddy-up, reindeer!' Thrilled by her own daring, she nudged her brother and whispered, 'I giddy-upped Father Christmas's reindeer!'

Stinkbomb, equally thrilled by the high-speed sleigh chase and pretending he was actually driving a really fast attack helicopter, grinned. 'I know,' he said, and made some helicopter noises.

'Right,' said Father Christmas. 'Hang on tight!' He flicked the reins, and the reindeer dropped into a steep dive, heading straight for the snowmobile.

'WHEEEEEEEEEEE!!!!!!'

Stinkbomb and Ketchup-Face yelled, their stomachs lurching delightfully, their thrilled eyes wide as the cold air rushed against their faces and the wide white moonlit ground rushed towards them.

'Wuurrrgh!!!'

roared the shopping trolleys, herding the badgers away from the trees.

'Faster, Rolf the Badger! Faster!!!' yelled Harry the Badger.

'AAAAAAAAARGH!!!'

he added, as the sleigh swooped out of the moonlit sky towards them.

Rolf the Badger jerked on the handlebars. The snowmobile slewed wildly across the snowy hillside. The sleigh swooped again; again the snowmobile skidded away. The fearsome shopping trolleys wuurrrghed their scary wuurrrgh at the terrified badgers.

The sleigh swooped, and the trolleys **wuurrrghed**, and the badgers **skidded** and

scooted and **slewed**. Soon the hillside was covered in snowmobile tracks, which looped and twirled and turned back on themselves, and at one point spelled out the word 'sausages' in very neat joined-up writing.

But it was hard to see how anyone could win the chase. The badgers couldn't escape from the swooping sleigh and the wuurrrgh-ing trolleys; but neither could our heroes bring an end to their badgery snowmobiling.

'How do we get them to stop?' Stinkbomb asked, as the sleigh rose into the sky again.

'Hmmm,' said Father Christmas, swinging the sleigh low over the shopping trolleys as they skied and slalomed in joyous pursuit of the snowmobile. 'I think I've just had an idea.' He fumbled in his pocket for a moment. 'Here!'

And he passed Ketchup-Face a small christ-massy orange.

'This is no time for a snack!' said Stinkbomb.

But Ketchup-Face was already taking off one of her snowshoes, and getting ready to serve.

❄   ❄   ❄

'Faster, Rolf the Badger! Faster!' shouted Harry the Badger.

'I'm fastering as fast as I can!' yelled Rolf the Badger. He pointed the snowmobile towards a particularly slopey part of the slope in the hope of further fastering his fastness—not seeing, behind him, the small round sleigh-to-badger missile hurtling towards them.

The perfectly-aimed orange smacked Rolf the Badger right in the bottom.

'Erk!' erked Rolf the Badger, losing control of the snowmobile . . .

. . . which skidded . . .

. . . slid . . .

144

... slipped ...

... slewed ...

... and shot at full speed up a particularly **big** snowdrift.

OOAAAAAA HHHHH!!!!!'

yelled the badgers, reaching the top and continuing upwards. The snowmobile turned somersaults in the air, spraying badgers in all directions.

'AAAAAAAARGH!!!'ₒₒₒ

they agreed, tumbling through the night sky.

'HEEEEELLL
LLLLPPPP!!!'ₒₒₒₒ

they added, raining down onto the shopping trolleys, who immediately invented the game of Catch
the Badger. For a moment, all that could be heard
was the gentle **rattling** and **thumping** and
ouching of trolleys catching badgers and badgers
being caught; and then the chase was over.

Father Christmas brought the sleigh to land. It glided to a gentle halt amongst the shopping trolleys, who all crowded round excitedly, eager to show him their cargoes of **groaning** badgers.

He smiled a **twinkling** smile at everyone, and laughed a merry 'Ho, ho, ho!' It was the exact opposite of an **evil** laugh, and the very sound of it filled Stinkbomb's and Ketchup-Face's hearts with joy and Christmassiness. 'Well,' he said, 'you've been very naughty badgers, and no mistake.'

The badgers shuffled uncomfortably. 'Er . . . have we?' one of them said, in an unconvincing attempt at innocence.

'Yes you have, you naughties!' Ketchup-Face said.

'You put Father Christmas in a sack and stopped him delivering presents!' Stinkbomb added.

'Oh. Was that naughty?' asked Stewart the Badger.

'Yes, it was!' said Father Christmas.

The badgers all looked guilty—probably because they *were* guilty.

'It was funny, though,' muttered Harry the Badger.

'Well,' said Father Christmas, 'I hope you're all going to go back to prison and think about your behaviour.'

'Yes, Father Christmas,' said the badgers gloomily.

'Is there anything else you'd like to say?' Father Christmas asked.

Stewart the Badger put his paw **up**. 'Could we have a digger for Christmas, please?'

'No you can't!' said Father Christmas firmly. 'Is there anything *else* you'd like to say?'

'Um . . . could we have a spade, then?' said Stewart the Badger.

'No!' said Father Christmas. 'Anything *else*???'

The badgers all stared gloomily at one another through the wires of the shopping trolleys, and then Rolf the Badger said, 'Um . . . sorry?'

'Oh, yeah!' said all the other badgers.

'Sorry!'

'Hmmm,' said Father Christmas. 'Well, don't do it again! Now, you shopping trolleys—you've all been very helpful. What would you like for Christmas?'

The shopping trolleys rattled sheepishly, and then the Queen of TrolleyHoliday™ trundled forwards a little and said, 'To be honest, your

Father Christmasness, we don't really celebrate Christmas. Sorry.'

Father Christmas chuckled. 'No need to apologize,' he said. 'Nobody *has* to celebrate Christmas. But would you like a present, anyway?'

The shopping trolleys muttered amongst themselves, and then the Queen said, 'Well . . . everybody likes presents . . . '

Father Christmas laughed once more. 'Very true!' he said. 'And once you've dropped those naughty badgers off in prison, you'll find some lovely . . . er . . . TrolleyHoliday™ presents waiting for you around the little Christmas tree in the Loose Chippings village square!'

'Oooh, *thank* you!' said all the shopping trolleys, and they turned and made for Loose Chippings as fast as their skis could carry them, leaving only Stinkbomb and Ketchup-Face with Father Christmas and his reindeer.

'Oh, my,' Father Christmas said, 'look at the time! I've got a lot of presents left to deliver. I don't suppose that you two would like to help, would you?'

Stinkbomb and Ketchup-Face just grinned, as they had never grinned before.

Chapter 17

In which there is a happy ending

It was early morning on Christmas Day on the little island of Great Kerfuffle. High above, the deep blue of night was growing pale. The bright moon was fading against the coming dawn. The light of the rising sun was spreading along the eastern horizon.

And in a tall tree in the garden of a lovely house high on a hillside above the tiny village of Loose Chippings, a blackbird was taking off its owl costume and getting ready to make a lot of noise.

And then it stopped and its lower beak dropped, as from high above came a magical sleigh pulled by eight magnificent reindeer, which drew to a halt upon the snow-covered lawn.

'Well,' said Father Christmas, 'all the presents have been safely delivered. Or . . . *almost* all.' He smiled: a jolly, **twinkly**, Christmassy smile. 'Just close your eyes and count to a hundred, will you?'

Stinkbomb and Ketchup-Face obediently closed their eyes; and Stinkbomb counted to one hundred while Ketchup-Face joined in with all her favourite numbers, but not necessarily in the right places.

'One hundred!' said Stinkbomb eventually.

'Seventy-four and a half!' added Ketchup-Face; and they both opened their eyes.

Father Christmas was nowhere to be seen. And neither was the sleigh, or the reindeer.

Ketchup-Face rubbed her eyes. 'Was it all a dream?' she asked, wonderingly.

'I don't think so,' said Stinkbomb. 'I'm pretty sure that last night we didn't go to sleep standing up in the garden. Come on—let's go and see if Father Christmas has been!'

They raced excitedly into the house—and stopped. For there, standing in front of the living-room door, was Malcolm the Cat. He looked as if he had just woken up, and there was still a light dusting of snow on his red soldier's jacket.

'Oh,' said Stinkbomb. 'Are you going to do your usual annoying thing of telling us we can't go in?'

'And changing your mind over and over again?' added Ketchup-Face.

'No, I'm not,'

said Malcolm the Cat; and then, as Stinkbomb

went to go past him, he added,

'Actually, I am.'

'But it's our house!' said Stinkbomb.

'No, it isn't,'
said Malcolm the Cat.

'Yes, it is!' said Stinkbomb.
'And it's Christmas!' added Ketchup-Face.

'No, it isn't,'
said Malcolm the Cat.

'Yes it is!' said Ketchup-Face.
'And anyway,' added Stinkbomb, 'we're nearly at the end of the story now.'

'No, we aren't,'
said Malcolm the Cat.

'Now you're just saying the opposite of everything we say!' said Stinkbomb.

'No, I'm not,'
said Malcolm the Cat.

'And it's really annoying!' said Ketchup-Face.

'No, it isn't,'
said Malcolm the Cat.

'Oh, do let them in, Malcolm the Cat,' said King Toothbrush Weasel's voice from behind the door. 'Everything's ready for them now.'

Malcolm the Cat reluctantly stood aside.

**Then he stood in front
of the door again.**

And then he stood aside again.

**And then he stood in front
of the door again.**

And in fact, this went on long enough for us to
go and take a look at the badgers.

❄   ❄   ❄

The badgers had fallen fast asleep after their long
night of **evil** and **wickedness**, almost as soon
as the shopping trolleys had dropped them off at
the jail. Now, with the first light of dawn creeping

through the prison bars, they were beginning to stir.

Stewart the Badger was the first to awaken properly. He sat up, yawned a little yawn—and then leapt to his paws excitedly, and shouted out:

'He's been! He's been!'

'We know he's been,' said Harry the Badger grumpily, without opening his eyes. 'He took us **UP** the chimney, remember?'

'No!' squeaked Stewart the Badger. 'I mean, he's been again!

And he's left us presents!!!'

'Presents?'

said all the other badgers, waking up suddenly.

It was true. The stockings that had hung so limply over the mantelpiece the night before were now plump and full. And underneath a tree—which none of them remembered having been there before—stood a cluster of brightly wrapped **presents**, one for each badger.

'Let's look in the stockings first!' said Harry the Badger excitedly, plunging his paw into his. 'It feels like chocolate money . . . and toys . . . and . . . um . . . an orange.'

'Awww,' said all the other badgers.

'Only kidding!' said Harry the Badger. 'It's worms!' And he pulled out a **wriggling** pawful.

'Yay! Worms!'

shouted all the other badgers excitedly, stuffing their paws into their own stockings.

'And what do you think these are?' Harry the Badger went on, looking at the brightly wrapped presents. They were all the same shape—a shape that could only be described as 'binny'.

'Hmmm . . . ' said Rolf the Badger happily. 'Shall we try knocking one over and see if it goes "**clang**"?'

'It's nice of Father Christmas to bring us all these **worms** and **dustbins**, isn't it!' said Stewart the Badger cheerfully.

'Well,' said Harry the Badger, 'we did say "sorry" . . .'

And there we must leave the badgers, happily digging pawfuls of worms out of their stockings and knocking over bin-shaped presents; for it was just around this point that Malcolm the Cat finally stopped standing in front of the door.

❄   ❄   ❄

Or rather, the door was swung open from inside the room, and there stood King Toothbrush Weasel. 'Come in, Stinkbomb and Ketchup-Face,' he said. 'You too, Malcolm the Cat.

The party's about to start!'

'Party?'

said Stinkbomb and Ketchup-Face, hurrying into the living-room; and then they stopped, eyes wide and bright and happy. For there, as well as King Toothbrush Weasel and Malcolm the Cat, was Miss Butterworth, and the little shopping trolley, and lots of other friends, too; and under the tree was a great stack of **presents** just waiting to be opened; and right in the middle of the gathering, looking large as life and twice as jolly, was Father Christmas himself.

'Ho, ho, ho!'

he laughed.

Christmas,

Ketchup-Face!

everybody!'

Stinkbomb and Ketchup-Face **smiled** the **smiliest smiles** they had ever **smiled**, their heads filled with memories of the night's adventure and their hearts filled with wonder and excitement; and thought that only one thing could make their happiness complete.

And then they heard footsteps coming **down** the stairs, and the living room door began to open again, and to their delight they saw two familiar shapes silhouetted in the doorway.

'HELLO, MY DARLINGS!'

came their mother's voice. 'Can we come in? Has the story finished yet?'

'Yes,' said Ketchup-Face happily.

'Would

like to

Christmas

you

play a

game?'

Play a Christmas game with Ketchup-Face!

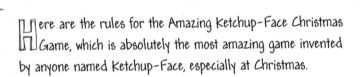

Here are the rules for the Amazing Ketchup-Face Christmas Game, which is absolutely the most amazing game invented by anyone named Ketchup-Face, especially at Christmas.

YOU NEED:

- A playing track

- A playing piece for every player

- This book. Or a different book if you can't find this one. But if you can't find this one you can't read how to play the game, so that would make it more difficult.

THE TRACK:

The easiest way to make the track is to tear up some used Christmas wrapping paper into big sort-of squares, write a number on each bit, and lay them in order on the floor. The longer the track is, the longer the game will go on. You probably need at least 20 squares. 427 would be too many.

THE PIECES:

The easiest way to make the pieces is for everybody to be their own playing piece and stand on the track. Make sure you make the track big enough. And don't put it on the table.

THE RULES:

Stand at the start. Each player takes it in turn to close their eyes, open the book at random, put their finger on the page, and then open their eyes and look at the word their finger has landed on. Count the number of letters in that word and then follow the instruction for that number:

THE INSTRUCTIONS:

If the number is **1**:
Dance around the room singing 'Cranberry Sauce'.
Then move one space forward.

If it's **2**: Get a lift three places ahead on a beautiful horsey named Starlight.

3. You are a badger. Say something silly and then go to prison. If there isn't a prison, go back to the start.

4. Let the youngest player go on to the square in front of you, if they want to. Even if you are the youngest player. And give them some chocolate, if you've got any.

5. Play a choosing game like 'Rock, Paper, Scissors' or 'Heads or Tails' with the person nearest you. The winner goes forward three places. The loser goes back three places. Unless the loser is the youngest player, in which case they can stay where they are.

6. Swap places with one of the other players. Enjoy the view from your new square. The youngest player can swap back again if they don't like it.

7. Get a lift on Santa's sleigh. Move forward FIVE WHOLE PLACES. Don't forget to giddy-up the reindeer.

**Yes you can!
No you can't!**

8. Ask Malcolm the Cat if you can move forward. Miss a go while you're waiting for him to make his mind up.

9. You are King Toothbrush Weasel. Command everyone else to go back two places. Don't forget to say 'please'.

10. It's Christmas! The person nearest you gets their head stuck in their stocking and misses the next go. Unless they're the youngest player, in which case they move forward one square.

Anything between **11** and a **million:** Shout 'Hey, look over there' and point out the window. Then sneakily move two squares forward while everyone's distracted.

Anything **more than a million:** The youngest player wins the game and becomes ruler of the universe and everyone has to bring them some cake.

Acknowledgements

To everyone—friends, family, and anyone else—who has been there with me, for me, or just near me this year.

MERRY CHRISTMAS!!!!

John Dougherty
(Author)

'Tis the season to write about badgers (again)

Photo © Michael Dannenberg

David Tazzyman
(Illustrator)

'Tis the season to draw badgers (again)

Illustration by Stanley Tazzyman

Ready for more great stories?

Try one of these . . .

More HO, HO, HO than Father Christmas!